APP

21st Century Skills **INNOVATION** Library

Radio

by Philip Brooks

INNOVATION IN **ENTERTAINMENT**

Cherry Lake Publishing

Published in the United States of America by Cherry Lake Publishing
Ann Arbor, Michigan
www.cherrylakepublishing.com

Content Adviser: Rick Morris, Associate Professor, Department of Radio/Television/Film, Northwestern University

Design: The Design Lab

Photo Credits: Cover and page 3, ©David R. Frazier Photolibrary, Inc./Alamy; page 5, ©iStockphoto.com/mrfotos; page 6, ©iStockphoto.com/track5; page 8, ©iStockphoto.com/CinematicFilm; page 9, ©Photo Researchers/Alamy; page 10, ©iStockphoto.com/egdigital; page 13, ©iStockphoto.com/swilmor; page 14, ©ClassicStock/Alamy; page 17, ©imagebroker/Alamy; page 18, ©AP Photo; page 20, ©iStockphoto.com/Petrovich9; page 23, ©iStockphoto.com/Macatack; page 24, ©North Wind Picture Archives/Alamy; page 25, ©Photo by: NBCU Photo Bank via AP Images; page 27, ©AP Photo/CBS, Inc.; page 28, ©AP Photo/XM Satellite Radio, Ron Thomas

Copyright ©2009 by Cherry Lake Publishing
All rights reserved. No part of this book may be reproduced or utilized in any form or by any means without written permission from the publisher.

Library of Congress Cataloging-in-Publication Data
Brooks, Philip.
 Radio / by Philip Brooks.
  p. cm.–(Innovation in entertainment)
 Includes index.
 ISBN-13: 978-1-60279-217-3
 ISBN-10: 1-60279-217-8
 1. Radio–Juvenile literature. I. Title. II. Series.
 TK6550.7.B74 2008
 621.384–dc22   2008008287

Cherry Lake Publishing would like to acknowledge the work of
The Partnership for 21st Century Skills.
Please visit www.21stcenturyskills.org *for more information.*

CONTENTS

Chapter One
Invisible Waves   4

Chapter Two
Sending Voices through the Air   8

Chapter Three
Radio as We Know It   12

Chapter Four
The Future of Radio   20

Chapter Five
Four Innovators   23

Glossary   30
For More Information   31
Index   32
About the Author   32

INNOVATION IN ENTERTAINMENT

CHAPTER ONE

Invisible Waves

"Bor-ing . . . ," Olivia complained on the drive home. "Can't we listen to something else?"

"What's wrong with National Public Radio?" her mom answered. "They have some interesting programs."

"How about some interesting *music* instead—and something from this decade, please," Olivia answered with a laugh.

"Oh, all right," said her mom, as she changed the radio channel. "But, you know, people didn't always have so many choices. And it wasn't so easy to get music and news like it is today."

"What do you mean?" Olivia replied. And her mother started to explain.

● ● ●

For thousands of years, human beings struggled to communicate across great distances. Before television and

Today, radio signals are sent through telecommunications towers and antennas.

radio, the **telegraph** was used to send simple messages hundreds of miles. But the telegraph solved only a tiny part of the communication puzzle. Telegraph wires were expensive and difficult to install. Also, messages had to be carried to people or printed in newspapers. Scientists wanted to find a method for sending messages without the use of wires.

By 1888, scientist Heinrich Rudolph Hertz proved the existence of invisible "radio" waves. Hertz discovered that an electric spark generates **electromagnetic** waves.

They behave much like ripples in water. He believed that a specially built **receiver** could detect these waves and turn them into sound. Many inventors thought the discovery of these waves might soon allow messages to be sent without the need for wires.

Various inventors built early versions of **transmitters** and receivers. In 1895, Italian inventor Guglielmo Marconi built equipment that allowed him to send wireless radio signals from one end of his house to the other. His system used a "spark-gap" transmitter. Electricity jumped a gap between two pieces of metal. The spark made radio waves that could be received as a pop or buzz heard on a pair of headphones.

This audio engineer listens to sound waves through headphones. The work of Guglielmo Marconi and others helped make this technology possible.

Marconi dreamed of being able to send wireless telegraphic messages instantly across the Atlantic Ocean. At first, he could only signal a few miles out. He continued to experiment. Later that year, he increased the length of the antennas he had built. Then he stood them up so they touched the ground. This "grounding" increased the signal's power.

In 1901, he built a powerful transmitter on the southwest tip of England. He also built a receiving station on the coast of Newfoundland. On December 12, 1901, he succeeded in sending the letter "s" in telegraphic code across the Atlantic Ocean. This was an achievement that would set the stage for the invention of radio and wireless communication.

Learning & Innovation Skills

Before the rise of companies such as General Electric Corporation (GE) and Radio Corporation of America (RCA), inventors worked alone or with a trusted assistant. As the 20th century dawned, corporations began hiring the best scientific minds out of colleges and universities. Many inventors became corporate professionals. Innovations often came faster as corporate scientists worked together. Of course, whatever these engineers and scientists invented belonged to the corporation. Today, most inventors must work with a team and learn to share credit for developing new technology.

CHAPTER TWO

Sending Voices through the Air

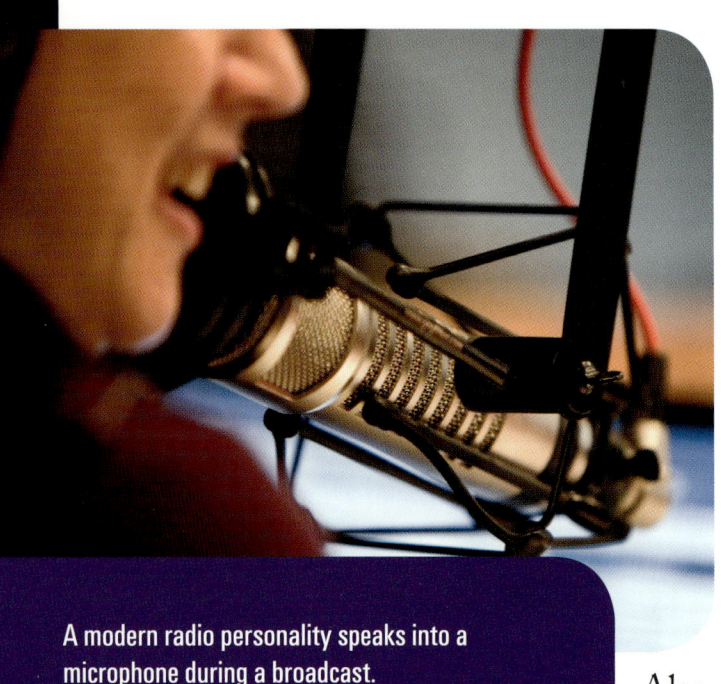

A modern radio personality speaks into a microphone during a broadcast.

By 1910, Marconi was running a profitable company sending telegraphic messages between Europe and the United States. But he had not invented radio as we know it today. A few technical puzzles still remained unsolved. For instance, Marconi's spark-gap transmitter could not send out the human voice. Also, radio receivers remained basic and had very limited sound quality. These were obstacles that many scientists would tackle over much of the 20th century.

Lee De Forest's inventions influenced the development of several industries including radio, film, and television. De Forest's vacuum tube made it possible to amplify radio waves.

Inventor Lee DeForest became obsessed with solving these problems. Building upon the work of others, DeForest designed a **vacuum tube** with two wires. He hoped that his new design would detect and **amplify** radio waves. When he added a third wire to the design in 1906, the tube worked. His "triode audion" improved clarity and volume in radio receivers. DeForest's work led to a basic version of **amplitude-modulated**, or AM, radio.

While DeForest was inventing the audion, Edwin Howard Armstrong was still a boy. As a teenager, Armstrong built a radio receiver and became obsessed with the new technology. He wanted to create better sound quality. In 1912, while still in his 20s, he perfected something he called a regenerative circuit. The device took signals created by DeForest's audion and sent them whirling 20,000 times through a circuit, or electric pathway. This process amplified the signals. Now, he could hear broadcasts from Honolulu, Hawaii, loud and clear in his Yonkers, New York, bedroom.

Early radios helped soldiers communicate with one another. Today, security guards use radios in a similar way.

Remarkably, Armstrong soon found that his new circuit could be used to transmit powerful and continuous radio waves. He constructed a huge antenna on top of his family home. He began making long-distance voice transmissions using his circuit in 1914. This meant the end of the old spark-gap transmitters. Armstrong also designed a device that allowed a receiver to be tuned to different frequencies, or channels.

The work of DeForest, Armstrong, and others thrilled radio hobbyists, who tinkered with the equipment and talked with one another. The military and railroads began using the new technology to communicate. Still, few people imagined a huge commercial future for the sale of radios or the broadcast of entertainment. But there was at least one teenager who decided that radio's future would be his life's work.

21st Century Content

During the early days of radio, anyone with a transmitter could broadcast at will. In 1934, the U.S. Congress established the Federal Communications Commission (FCC) to bring order to the chaos. Today, the FCC licenses and regulates communications by radio, television, wire, satellite, and cable. It makes decisions about who owns the airwaves. The FCC also decides what content is acceptable for broadcasting. FCC decisions often raise controversy. Deciding who is allowed to broadcast helps decide whose opinions get heard. In addition, some people feel that the FCC bans or revises too much material. Others feel that the agency allows too much inappropriate material to be aired.

CHAPTER THREE

Radio as We Know It

In 1906, 15-year-old David Sarnoff took a job with Marconi's telegraph company. When Marconi met the new kid in the office, he was immediately impressed. Sarnoff steadily moved up the company's ladder. On April 14, 1912, Sarnoff was operating Marconi's telegraph station on top of a department store in New York. He picked up a telegraphed message that stunned the world: "S.S. *Titanic* ran into iceberg, sinking fast." For the next 72 hours, Sarnoff and several others remained in the station. They passed along news of the disaster, including names of survivors.

Young Sarnoff spent his spare time studying electronics at the library and talking with radio technicians. His technical knowledge grew, and he had a strong business sense. In 1915, he submitted an idea for

Radio as We Know It

David Sarnoff had the idea for a "radio music box" like this one.

a "radio music box" to his bosses at Marconi's company. Sarnoff wrote that his idea would "bring music into the house by wireless." He imagined radio stations on the air with good programs. Then Marconi could build radios and sell them to every American family.

Executives at the company dismissed the idea. But Sarnoff knew they were wrong. In 1919, General Electric Corporation bought Marconi's company. Sarnoff got a chance to pitch his idea to the newly formed Radio Corporation of America (RCA). He insisted that the new company should build and sell radios not just to hobbyists who liked gizmos, but to average Americans. He explained the key to promoting sales of radio sets. RCA would need to create radio stations that provided entertainment for the whole family.

As a demonstration of his plan, Sarnoff helped arrange the broadcast of a big boxing match in 1921.

During the 1930s and 1940s, many families sat together and listened to the radio each evening.

The event captured the imagination of sports fans. About 300,000 people heard the broadcast. RCA soon sold thousands of its Radiolas for about $75 each. Radio stations popped up everywhere. Radio had arrived.

Once radio's basic technology was in place, the next innovations came in its **programming**. Music and news dominated the dial. Soon, sporting events took over the radio waves. Radio's popularity began to grow heading into the 1930s. The Great Depression hit the American economy hard in 1929. It was a grim time. Radio became the way in which Americans received news about the economy. People turned to radio entertainment to try to forget about the Depression. Many of the biggest names in show business began performing on the radio.

These creative minds built radio into a major entertainment industry. But comedy and drama had to be reinvented for the new **medium**. At a play or movie, audiences could see the actors. Radio required stories to be told in ways that created pictures in listeners' minds. During the early 1930s, a few pioneers created methods of storytelling that others imitated and built upon.

The comedy **serial** *Amos & Andy* was the earliest nationwide hit on radio. In 1930 and 1931, nearly one-third of all Americans—about 40 million people—tuned in to hear the latest episode. Charles Correll and Freeman Gosden, two white men, portrayed Amos and

Andy, a pair of African Americans. The characters, though much loved, were based on racial **stereotypes**. If you listen to an old clip of the program today, it may sound strange and even offensive.

Correll and Gosden played a big part in the invention of radio comedy. *Amos & Andy* was aired six days a week. So Correll and Gosden decided that their scripts should include plots and subplots. That way, they could twist and turn the story to last over many shows. To bring listeners back for more each day, they made sure each show ended with a suspenseful moment, a "cliff-hanger." Correll and Gosden also figured out how to make themselves wealthy. They "syndicated" their program. This meant they didn't just broadcast their show once a day over a single network. Instead, they recorded it and sold copies to any local station willing to pay them a fee. This method of selling programs soon caught on.

As radio sets entered most homes in America, cleaning-product manufacturers saw an opportunity. They wanted to **sponsor** programs aimed at housewives. But what sort of programming did women want? In 1930, a woman named Irna Phillips was working for WGN radio in Chicago. Her bosses asked her to create a program about "a family." She wrote a drama she called *Painted Dreams*. It was radio's first "soap opera." The show featured long-running characters. Listeners came

> Modern radio shows include interviews, which are much different from the early shows.

to care about these characters as if they were friends or neighbors. Phillips chose a slow narrative pace so that if a busy mother missed a few minutes or even the entire program, she could quickly catch up. She also used suspenseful endings to leave listeners wanting more. She used organ music to heighten emotional moments in the show and to move from one scene to the next. All these ideas were borrowed by competing shows.

By March 1933, radio had become a central part of American life. At this time, many Americans were affected by the Great Depression. They were losing faith in the government. President Franklin D. Roosevelt became the first president to take full advantage of radio's power. He brought his voice directly into citizens' homes. Roosevelt gave a series of evening radio talks designed to help calm Americans' fear of the Depression. He decided to speak in a quiet, casual style that he believed would be fitting for the new medium. "My friends," he said, "I want to tell you what has been done in the last few days, why it has been done, and what the next steps are going

During the Great Depression, U.S. president Franklin D. Roosevelt reassured the nation with his radio broadcast "fireside chats."

to be." The friendly talks helped reassure and unite the nation. These radio broadcasts became known as "fireside chats."

Radio brought World War II (1939–1941) closer to Americans than the previous world war (1914–1918). The most famous and innovative war correspondent was Edward R. Murrow. He moved radio directly into the action, broadcasting live from London during the summer and fall of 1940. Murrow and his team of reporters were the first to broadcast a show live from multiple locations at once. Americans could hear the sounds of war. These included the footsteps of Londoners hurrying to bomb shelters and the deep thuds and booms of German bombs hitting the city. Radio expanded people's access to information across the world.

Learning & Innovation Skills

Long before people owned computers, cell phones, or even fax machines, David Sarnoff envisioned them all. In 1964, a time when most Americans still did not have color TV sets, he said:

"The computer will become the hub of a vast network of remote data stations and information banks.... Eventually, a global communications network... will instantly link man to machine—or machine to machine.... [The computer] will affect man's ways of thinking, his means of education, his relationship to his physical and social environment, and it will alter his ways of living."

How much of Sarnoff's vision of the future do you recognize today? Can you imagine new ways in which technology will change the way people live 40 years from now?

INNOVATION IN ENTERTAINMENT

CHAPTER FOUR

The Future of Radio

Communications satellites that are orbiting Earth send digital signals for today's satellite radio.

Today, television and the Internet have replaced radio as the most popular media in American homes. This has not stopped radio innovation. Hugh Panero was an early developer of cable television. In the 1990s, he began thinking of how he might get people to begin paying for radio as they did for cable TV. He thought that radio stations had too many commercials and had forgotten about music lovers. What if subscribers to his radio company could get hundreds of channels with a huge variety of commercial-free music and talk programming?

Panero and his technicians soon came to believe that the future of radio was in outer space. Most people listened to the radio while driving. A satellite broadcast could come in loud and clear no matter where you took your car. Signals sent from above Earth would not grow weak as you drove far from a radio tower or traveled through hills or mountains.

They planned the launch of satellites. They also built specialized microchips to allow listeners to receive the signals. Panero named the company XM. In spring 2001, XM launched two satellites, named "Rock" and "Roll." Another company, Sirius Satellite Radio, began broadcasting in July 2002. Other companies soon sprang up. In 2007, Sirius Satellite Radio and XM announced plans to join the two companies together. This is a business move known as a merger.

> **Life & Career Skills**
>
> Hugh Panero was able to see new ways to use radio technology even though many people thought TV and the Internet were the wave of the future. Many 21st century innovators will be people who can see different uses for a product or technology. They will be the people able to adapt products to the changing needs and desires of customers.

21st Century Content

Internet technology makes it possible for people around the world to communicate with one another in ways that the early inventors of radio technology couldn't even imagine. Satellite radio waves travel through space, but Internet radio doesn't use radio waves at all. Instead, digital data is "streamed." That means it is broken into bits, sent over cable or telephone lines, and put back together a moment later by a listener's computer. Many standard radio stations stream their programming and can be heard anywhere on Earth by anyone with access to the World Wide Web.

A podcast is a digital media file that can be downloaded via the Internet. Downloaded files can be saved to a portable media player for listening on the move. "Podcasters" can sell their content or give it away. Many offer subscriptions.

Today, many cars are equipped with satellite radio receivers. Satellite radio companies expect to have more than 20 million U.S. subscribers by 2010. Satellite radio companies do research to find out what kinds of radio programs people like. Then they create stations tailored to their subscribers' tastes in music.

What does the future hold for radio? No one knows for sure. But creative thinkers in the industry are sure to keep us entertained through the 21st century and beyond.

CHAPTER FIVE

Four Innovators

Many innovators have contributed to the growth of radio. The following are the stories of four people who have helped shape the radio industry.

Guglielmo Marconi

Guglielmo Marconi was born in Bologna, Italy, in 1874. His father was a wealthy Italian nobleman, and his mother was from a wealthy family in Ireland. As a boy, Gugleilmo was

Many modern radios are small enough to fit in a pocket.

INNOVATION IN ENTERTAINMENT

Gugleilmo Marconi first successfully transmitted a wireless signal in 1895.

fascinated by electricity. He studied books by scientists and engineers. At age 21, he began experimenting with wireless telegraphy.

In 1896, he loaded his "wireless telegraphy system" onto a ship and headed to England. There he was granted a patent, which is a license to make an invention. In 1909, Marconi was awarded a Nobel Prize for his work on radio technology—the highest honor a scientist can receive. He died in Rome, Italy, on July 20, 1937.

As television became popular in the 1950s, Irna Phillips brought several of her radio shows to TV and created new soap operas.

Irna Phillips

Irna Phillips was born in Chicago in 1901. She grew up in poverty and dreamed of becoming a famous actress. She once described herself as "a plain, sickly, silent child, with hand-me-down clothes and no friends."

She attended college at Northwestern University and studied drama. When teachers convinced her she was not pretty enough to be a stage actress, she became a teacher instead. Soon, she left teaching and took work at Chicago's WGN radio station as an actress and announcer.

Phillips created *Painted Dreams*, radio's first soap opera. She wrote and acted on the show until 1932. She left the station after a disagreement over who owned the program. She headed for a rival station and created a show called *Today's Children*. It was strikingly similar to *Painted Dreams*. By 1943, Phillips had five programs on the air at once. It has been estimated that she wrote at least 2 million words a year at her peak. Phillips died on December 22, 1973.

Edward R. Murrow

Many people consider Edward R. Murrow the greatest hero of American broadcast journalism. Murrow was born near Greensboro, North Carolina, in 1908. Brought up in a strict Quaker household, he was devoted to the pursuit of truth and justice. He began as a radio reporter in 1935. He wrote his own scripts and created a powerful, plainspoken style. He soon became more than a reporter, speaking out against evil wherever he saw it. Writer David Halberstam once wrote that Murrow was

Four Innovators   27

Edward R. Murrow was well known for his radio broadcasts before he started working in television in 1951.

"one of those rare legendary figures who was as good as his myth." Murrow made the jump to television, but he claimed that radio remained his first love. Known to be a heavy smoker, he died of lung cancer in New York in 1965.

INNOVATION IN ENTERTAINMENT

Hugh Panero

Hugh Panero, founder of XM Radio, began his career as a journalist. He was once turned down for a job reporting about cable television for a magazine devoted to the industry. But he did not give up. He created his own version of the publication, complete with a snazzy

Hugh Panero shows off the control room at XM Satellite Radio headquarters in Septermber 2001.

cover and filled with stories he wrote. He hoped his own magazine would rival the magazine that turned him down. He faced similar obstacles while helping to build the cable television industry.

When he began work at Time Warner Cable of New York City, many argued no one would pay for cable television. After all, they could get broadcast shows for free. Panero never doubted that better programming would bring subscribers. He was right. When he began work on XM radio in 1998, the same belief in programming guided his decisions and proved correct once more.

Learning & Innovation Skills

Even today, various nations claim to be the home of "the father of radio." Italy has Marconi. Russians celebrate May 7 as Radio Day in honor of inventor Alexander Popov. In India, many consider Jagadish Chandra Bose to be radio's inventor. Serbs remind Italians that the U.S. Supreme Court supported claims that electrical engineer Nikola Tesla—rather than Marconi—owns key radio patents.

All are interesting and brilliant men. They all seem to have created transmitters and receivers of varying capabilities at about the same time. The question becomes one of exact dates and what you mean when you say "invent" and "radio." How would you go about deciding who invented radio?

INNOVATION IN ENTERTAINMENT

Glossary

amplify (AM-pli-fye) to make something louder or stronger

amplitude-modulated (AM-pli-tood MAH-joo-lay-tid) a frequency or format of radio, known mostly as AM radio

electromagnetic (i-lek-troh-mag-NEH-tick) relating to a temporary magnet created by running electricity through a wire coil

medium (MEE-dee-uhm) a means for communicating to a large number of people

programming (PROH-gram-eeng) television- or radio-show scheduling

receiver (ri-SEE-vur) equipment that receives radio or television signals

serial (SIHR-ee-uhl) a story that is told in several parts on radio or television

sponsor (SPON-sur) to pay the costs of a radio or television program in return for having your product advertised

stereotypes (STER-ee-oh-tipes) overly simplified pictures of, or opinions about, people or groups of people

telegraph (TEH-luh-graf) a device that is part of a communication system in which electrical signals are used to send messages over wires

transmitters (transs-MIT-uhrz) devices that send out radio or television signals

vacuum tube (VAH-kyoom TOOB) a glass tube, surrounding an area from which all gases have been removed, that can be used to modify an electrical signal

For More Information

BOOKS

Fedunkiw, Marianne. *Inventing the Radio*. New York: Crabtree Children's Books, 2007.

Woods, Mary B., and Michael Woods. *The History of Communication*. Minneapolis: Lerner Publications, 2005.

Zannos, Susan. *Guglielmo Marconi and the Story of Radio Waves*. Hockessin, DE: Mitchell Lane Publishers, 2004.

WEB SITES

Ken Burns American Stories: *Empire of the Air: The Men Who Made Radio*.
www.pbs.org/kenburns/empire
A PBS web site describing a fascinating special by Ken Burns about the history of radio and television communications

The FCC Kids Zone—Radio FAQs
www.fcc.gov/cgb/kidszone/faqs_radio.html
An FCC site for kids that answers common questions about radios and how they work

Index

AM (amplitude-modulated) radio, 9
Amos & Andy radio show, 15–16
antennas, 7, 11
Armstrong, Howard, 10–11

Bose, Jagadish Chandra, 29

"cliff-hangers," 16, 17
commercials, 21
Correll, Charles, 16

DeForest, Lee, 9, 10

electromagnetic waves, 4–5, 6, 9, 11, 15, 22
entertainment, 11, 13–15, 15–17

Federal Communications Commission (FCC), 11
"fireside chats," 19
frequencies, 11

General Electric Corporation (GE), 7, 13
Gosden, Freeman, 16
Great Depression, 15, 18–19
grounding, 7

Halberstam, David, 26–27
Hertz, Heinrich Rudolph, 4
hobbyists, 11, 14

Internet, 20, 21, 22

Marconi, Guglielmo, 5–7, 8, 12, 23–24, 29
mergers, 21
military, 11
MP3 players. See portable media players.
Murrow, Edward R., 19, 26–27
music, 13, 15, 17, 21, 22

news, 12, 15, 19, 26
Nobel Prize, 24

Painted Dreams radio show, 17, 26
Panero, Hugh, 20–21, 28–29
patents, 24, 29
Phillips, Irna, 16–17, 25–26
podcasts, 22
Popov, Alexander, 29
portable media players, 22

Radio Corporation of America (RCA), 7, 13–14
Radio Day, 29
Radiolas, 15
radio shows, 15–16, 17, 26
radio stations, 13, 14, 15, 16, 20–21, 22, 26
radio waves, 4–5, 6, 9, 11, 15, 22
railroads, 11
receivers, 4, 5, 8, 9, 10, 11, 29
regenerative circuits, 10–11
Roosevelt, Franklin D., 18–19

Sarnoff, David, 12–15, 19
satellite radio, 11, 20–22, 28
serials, 15–16
Sirius Satellite Radio, 21
soap operas, 16–17, 26
"spark-gap" transmitters, 6, 8, 11
sporting events, 14–15
streaming, 22
syndication, 16

telegraph, 4, 12, 24
television, 11, 20, 21, 27, 29
Tesla, Nikola, 29
Time Warner Cable, 29
Today's Children radio show, 26
transmitters, 5, 6, 7, 8, 11, 29
triode audion, 9, 10

vacuum tubes, 9

World War II, 19

XM Radio, 21, 28, 29

About the Author

Philip Brooks is a freelance writer living in Brooklyn, New York, with his wife, Balinda, and son, Felix. He has published many other children's books as well as fiction for adults.